OKOMI
The New Baby

Helen and
Clive Dorman

Illustrated by
Tony Hutchings

Dawn Publications
in association with The Jane Goodall Institute

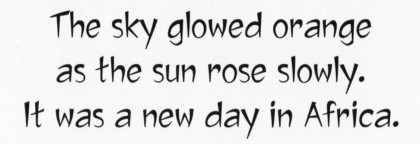

The sky glowed orange
as the sun rose slowly.
It was a new day in Africa.

Deep in the forest the leaves
on the trees were bright
with morning dew.

The chimpanzees were
waking from their night's
sleep in the treetops.

All except one.
Mama Du had been missing
from the family group
for two days.

Where had she gone?

Hunched up on a bed of leaves by
a nearby tree, sat Mama Du.
Her dark coat was coppery-brown
in the sunlight.

She had been away,
but now she was back.

She looked tired.

A butterfly fluttered past
Mama Du's nose.
Her eyes opened.

She looked down at
a tiny, furry bundle.
Who was asleep in her lap?

It was her new baby
—Baby Okomi!

His face was small and wrinkled.
He was fast asleep.

Slowly, Okomi yawned.
First he opened one eye.
Then he opened the other.

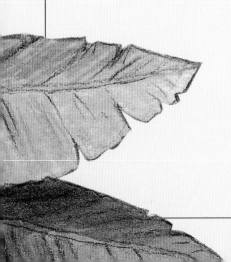

Okomi looked up at his mommy,
Mama Du.

She was fascinated by his
wrinkly, pink face
and beautiful big brown eyes.

Mama Du reached out and
stroked Okomi's cheek.
Okomi reached out and tried to
touch Mama Du's nose.
But he missed!

Mama Du grunted quietly.
She was very proud of Okomi
and cuddled him close to her.

A new baby in the
family group always causes
great excitement.
Mama Du was an important
female, so Okomi was
an important baby.

One of the chimpanzees swung
down to the ground.
She saw Mama Du holding the
tiny baby and grunted softly.

Soon, everyone heard the news
and all the chimpanzees
gathered around Mama Du to
see and try to touch Okomi.

Although Mama Du was proud
of her little baby, she was not
happy with so many onlookers.

Suddenly a large male
chimpanzee came crashing
through the trees.
The rest of the chimpanzees
scattered.

It was Dada Du—the biggest and
strongest chimpanzee.

He had come to see, too.

Dada Du sat next to Mama Du
and peered at their son.
She groomed Dada Du to show
him he was welcome to stay.

Dada Du lay down.
He reached out and gently
touched Okomi as they all
relaxed in the sunshine.

Okomi is very lucky to have
such a close family.

The Work Of Jane Goodall

Photo by Michael Neugebauer

For many years, Jane Goodall patiently watched chimpanzees in the African forest. She saw chimp babies play with their mothers and that chimpanzees have close family ties. She saw young chimps throw tantrums and have exciting learning adventures. She saw that the chimpanzee mother-infant relationship is virtually identical to its human counterpart.

Jane Goodall's research of more than 40 years showed how chimpanzees reason and solve problems, how they make tools and use them, and how they communicate. It revealed that they have a wide range of emotions. It showed that each of them has a unique, vivid personality. Indeed, their genetic makeup is closer to us than any other animal—with almost 99% identical DNA. Jane's revolutionary work bids us to look upon chimpanzees as non-human relatives.

Jane with an orphan chimpanzee

Photo by Michael Neugebauer

Yet the plight of these "relatives" is desperate. Their forests are being cut down. They are being hunted for food. Their numbers are dwindling drastically. And when chimpanzee mothers are killed, the orphaned babies—often taken to be sold illegally as pets—cannot be returned successfully to the wild.

When Jane realized that chimpanzees were becoming endangered, she began a worldwide effort on their behalf. She campaigns tirelessly, and established The Jane Goodall Institute. It has created sanctuaries for orphan chimpanzees. (You can help the orphans by "adopting a chimp.") It works to improve conditions in zoos and laboratories, and to halt deforestation and the bushmeat trade. The Institute also

Fanni and her baby, Fax.

sponsors Roots & Shoots, a worldwide program for young people working to make a difference for animals, the environment and their communities. For more information contact The Jane Goodall Institute, P.O. Box 14890, Silver Spring, MD 20910, or call (301) 565-0086, or go to www.janegoodall.org.

Part of the proceeds from the sale of this book supports the work of The Jane Goodall Institute's Tchimpounga Sanctuary in the Congo Republic. Dawn Publications is dedicated to inspiring in children a deeper understanding and appreciation for all life on Earth. To view our full list of titles, or to order, please visit our web site at www.dawnpub.com, or call 800-545-7475.